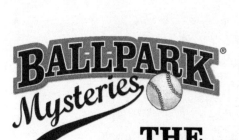

THE
WORLD
SERIES
KIDS

BALLPARK MYSTERIES®

Also by David A. Kelly
THE MVP SERIES

Babe Ruth and the Baseball Curse

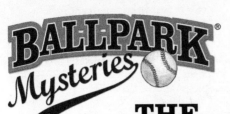

SUPER
SPECIAL
#4

THE
WORLD
SERIES
KIDS

by David A. Kelly

illustrated by Mark Meyers

A STEPPING STONE BOOK™
Random House 🏠 New York

*This book is dedicated to the players and coaches of
the West Newton, Massachusetts, Little League.*
—D.A.K.

*You're playing a game, whether it's Little League or Game 7
of the World Series. It's impossible to do well unless you're having
a good time. People talk about pressure. Yeah, there's pressure.
But I just look at it as fun.*
—Derek Jeter, shortstop for the New York Yankees

Text copyright © 2019 by David A. Kelly
Cover art and interior illustrations copyright © 2019 by Mark Meyers

All rights reserved. Published in the United States by Random House Children's Books, a division of Penguin Random House LLC, New York.

Random House and the colophon are registered trademarks and A Stepping Stone Book and the colophon are trademarks of Penguin Random House LLC. Ballpark Mysteries® is a registered trademark of Upside Research, Inc.

Visit us on the Web!
rhcbooks.com

Educators and librarians, for a variety of teaching tools,
visit us at RHTeachersLibrarians.com

Library of Congress Cataloging-in-Publication Data
Names: Kelly, David A. (David Andrew), author. | Meyers, Mark, illustrator.
Title: The World Series kids / by David A. Kelly; illustrated by Mark Meyers.
Description: New York: Random House, [2019] | Series: Ballpark mysteries. Super special; #4 | "A Stepping Stone book."
Summary: Cousins Mike and Kate investigate when someone tries to stop the Cooperstown team from participating in the Little League World Series in Williamsport, Pennsylvania.
Identifiers: LCCN 2018042255 | ISBN 978-0-525-57895-6 (trade) |
ISBN 978-0-525-57896-3 (lib. bdg.) | ISBN 978-0-525-57897-0 (ebook)
Subjects: | CYAC: Baseball—Fiction. | Little League World Series (Baseball)—Fiction. | Sabotage—Fiction. | Conduct of life—Fiction. | Williamsport (Pa.)—Fiction. | Mystery and detective stories.
Classification: LCC PZ7.K2936 Wor 2019 | DDC [Fic]—dc23

Printed in the United States of America
10 9 8 7 6 5 4 3 2 1

This book has been officially leveled by using the F&P Text Level Gradient™ Leveling System.

Contents

A Slashing Development

"Cowabunga!" Mike Walsh called out.

He ran along the top of a grassy hill holding a long piece of a sturdy cardboard box in front of him. At the edge, Mike jumped chest first onto the cardboard and rode it like a sled all the way to the bottom of the hill!

"Woo-hoo!" Mike's cousin Kate Hopkins called out. "Watch out below!" Kate jumped on her own piece of cardboard and flew down the hill.

But just as she reached the bottom, a TV reporter wandered into her path.

"Oh no!" Kate yelled. "Get out of the way!"

The TV reporter was too busy talking to the camera to hear Kate's yell. Kate tried to pull the sled to the left.

"Look out!" Kate cried.

The TV reporter spun around. Kate was only feet away! The reporter jerked his right leg up and lost his balance. Kate shot underneath his raised foot with only inches to spare! The TV reporter tottered sideways and then belly-flopped to the ground.

Kate slid to a halt a few feet away.

"Wow, that was close!" Kate said as she sprang up from the cardboard. "Are you okay?"

The TV reporter rolled over. He picked up his microphone, stood up, and dusted some grass off his pants. "Yes, I am," he said. He glanced up the hill at the other kids sledding on pieces of cardboard. "I was looking for action shots for our show tomorrow. But that was a little *too* much action!"

"Don't worry, Matt, we have it all on video! Your belly flop will make a great opening to tomorrow's show!" a gruff-looking cameraman said from the sidewalk. "I can see it now: 'The Agony of Defeat!'"

Mike and Kate were at Lamade Stadium in South Williamsport, Pennsylvania, for the Little League Baseball World Series. The event was held there each year. It brought the best eight teams from across the United States together with the best eight teams from regions around the world. Players had to be between ten and twelve years old.

The series would start the next day. Mike

3

and Kate had driven down from their home in Cooperstown, New York, that morning with Kate's mother, Mrs. Hopkins. She was a sports reporter for American Sportz. She was covering that year's series.

Matt the TV reporter smiled. "I don't know about using that video," he said. "I'd never hear the end of it!" He turned to Kate. "I should have been paying more attention. I'm sorry to get in your way."

Kate shrugged. "It's okay!" she said. "At least you lifted up your leg so I didn't hit you!"

"Yeah!" Mike said. "Because if you hadn't, it really would have been the agony of da-feet! Get it? Da feet? The feet?"

Kate groaned.

"Well, we're lucky everyone is okay," Matt said. "But if you'll excuse me, we've got to get back to work." He waved to Mike and Kate and headed off.

Mike nudged Kate. "Hey, where's Colin?" he asked. "It's after four o'clock—he's late! If his team doesn't get here soon, they'll miss the big parade tonight!"

The night before the series kicked off, all the teams rode on floats in a giant parade in downtown Williamsport. Their friend Colin's team from Cooperstown had beaten all the other teams in New York State and the Mid-Atlantic Region to make it to the series. Mike and Kate hadn't made the team.

Kate glanced around. Lots of kids were sledding down the hill on pieces of cardboard. There was no sign of Colin or the Cooperstown team.

"I don't see him anywhere," Kate said. "But

look at that!" She pointed to the sidewalk on the far side of the hill. A small dog was racing around in circles while an older woman tried to catch it.

"Let's go get it!" Mike said.

When Kate and Mike ran over, the dog barked happily and sprang to its left. As Kate reached for it, Mike stepped on the dog's leash.

"Gotcha!" Mike said.

"You did it!" the woman said. "Thank you

for catching my dog, Charlie. He's too fast for me!"

Mike handed her the leash. "You're welcome," he said. "I'm glad we could help."

The woman fished around in her pocket and pulled her hand out. "Here," she said. "I'd like you two to have this, since you took the time to help me."

She dropped a colorful pin into Mike's outstretched hand. The pin was shaped like an open baseball glove. The word *Founder* was written across its front in silver script. "Oh cool, it's a Little League World Series pin," Mike said. "Thanks." He tried to hand it back to her. "But you really don't have to. Kate and I were happy to help catch Charlie!"

The woman waved him off. "Please, take the pin for helping me," she said. "You can bring it to the pin-trading area tomorrow and swap it for a different pin if you want. It's a special pin and should be easy to trade. But Charlie and I have to get home for supper now." The woman tugged on Charlie's leash, and they walked off the other way.

"Our first Little League pin!" Kate said. "I wonder why it's special. Maybe we can trade it for two pins tomorrow, one for each of us!"

"Great idea," Mike said. As he slipped the pin into his pocket, he noticed a group of kids at the top of the hill near the main entrance gate.

"Hey, that looks like Colin's team!" Mike said.

He and Kate sprinted to the main gate. The team had just stepped off a big yellow school bus. Kate spotted Colin, and she and Mike ran over to him.

"What happened?" Kate asked. "Why were you so late? You were supposed to race us on the sledding hill!"

Colin shook his head. "I know," he said. "But when we stopped to eat at a rest stop, we were stranded! Someone slit the tires on our bus!"

Caught in the Grove

"When we came out of the rest stop to get back on the bus, half the tires were flat!" Colin said. "The replacement bus took a long time to get there. We were worried we'd miss the parade!"

"Who slit the tires?" Kate asked.

"I don't know, but Coach Caleb's son, Zach, saw them," Colin said. Colin pointed to a college-aged red-haired boy carrying a backpack and wearing a Cooperstown jersey.

"Do you remember Zach?" Colin asked.

"He was the star of the last Cooperstown team to go to the Little League World Series. That was ten years ago. They didn't make it to the finals, but they set the record for the biggest comeback ever! Zach's team was down by twelve runs but still managed to win the game. He drove in seven of the thirteen runs with his special hitting technique that he calls Big Daddy Hacks!"

"I've always wanted to learn how to hit the ball like him," Mike said. He swung a pretend bat. "I think with Big Daddy Hacks you swing down in a chopping motion. It's supposed to make the ball go farther."

"But isn't Zach a little old to be on your team?" Kate asked.

Colin laughed. "He's just helping his dad by managing our equipment," he said. "We keep trying to get him to give us Big Daddy Hacks hitting lessons, but he doesn't want to share his secret. Hey, Zach!" Colin called out. "Tell my friends Mike and Kate what happened at the rest stop!"

Zach turned around and smiled. He pushed through the clump of boys to make his way over to Mike, Kate, and Colin.

"It was unbelievable!" Zach said. A few of the other players paused to listen. "I went out to the bus to get my wallet. I heard a strange hissing sound from the other side of the bus, so I ran around and saw a teenager sticking a knife into the front tire! When he spotted me, he yelled, 'You guys are going to lose!'

Then he jumped over the guardrail and into the woods. I tried to catch him but lost him in the trees."

"Did you see what he looked like?" Mike asked.

Zach shook his head. "Not really. He was a teenager, about my height. Thin. He had a neon green T-shirt on," he said. "It seemed like he was out to hurt the team. It didn't seem like a prank."

"Maybe fans of the other teams are jealous!" said a voice from behind them.

Mike and Kate turned around. It was Matt, the TV reporter who Kate had almost plowed into earlier. He stepped forward and put a microphone in front of Zach.

"Your team is the clear favorite to win the series," Matt continued. "Someone might be trying to level the playing field! How will the

Cooperstown team hold up under this type of pressure?"

Zach's dad, Coach Caleb, stepped up and patted the shoulders of his nearby players. "This team is strong," he said. "I think they're going to do a great job out there, *even* if someone doesn't want them to win!"

"Well, our viewers are looking for an exciting series," Matt continued. "If you guys just cruise through the tournament, I don't know if anyone will watch the games. It would be more thrilling if you lost a game."

Coach Caleb waved his hand. "We're here to play our best baseball," he said. "But we've got to get going to prepare for the parade, right, kids?"

"Yay! Let's go!" the team called out. They surged forward to the entrance of the International Grove. The Grove was the housing area where the teams and coaches lived during the series. Mike and Kate grabbed Colin's backpack and walked along with him.

Since the team was so late, the security guards just waved them into the living compound. The kids walked through the tall black iron gates and headed for the main player housing buildings. The two-story buildings were painted brown and had red, white, and blue banners hanging from their porches.

"Wow! This is amazing!" Mike said as the team walked into a huge game room.

The kids dropped their bags and scattered to explore. Pinball machines and arcade games lined one wall. A group of international players from Japan and Australia were playing spirited games of Ping-Pong in the middle of the room. A bunch of players in the green and red uniforms of the Mexico

team were lounging on couches and watching sports on the giant video screen. A girl with long hair waved to the newcomers.

Kate waved back. *"¡Hola!"* she said. "Hello!" She was teaching herself Spanish. She liked to practice when she could. *"¡Bienvenida!* Welcome!"

Colin looked around. "And this is only the game room," he said. "There's supposed to be a swimming pool outside and a cafeteria that has all kinds of great food! I heard there's even a freezer where you can get free ice cream!"

"I know who would like that," Kate said.

Mike licked his lips and lifted Colin's baseball bag. "I am kinda hungry from helping carry all this stuff," he said.

Kate nudged Mike. "Hey, I don't think we're allowed to have free ice cream," she said.

"We're not even supposed to be inside the Grove since we're not on the team!"

Mike nodded. "I know," he said. "But it's okay, we're *with* the team." He held up Colin's bag again. "We're helping the team unload!"

Mike pulled a baseball out of his pocket. He carried a ball with him wherever he went. He made a motion like a pitcher. "Plus, if they ask what I'm doing here, I can say I'm a relief pitcher!" he said.

"But you're not that good at pitching," Kate said. "You said so last week."

"Yeah, I know," Mike said. "That's why it's a *relief* that I'm not the pitcher!"

Kate rolled her eyes and glanced out the window. "Hey, look at the swimming pool!" she said. She walked over to a window overlooking a big green lawn. In the middle of the grass was a giant pool. Kids from different teams were taking turns doing cannonballs to see who could make the biggest splash.

Colin and Mike moved over to the windows, too. Mike started to take his shirt off. "I'll bet I could easily make the biggest splash," he said. "Just wait until I get out there."

Before Mike could head for the door, a hand slapped down on his shoulder.

"The only splash you're going to make is when you walk back through those security gates," a voice said. "Because you two are not supposed to be in here!"

A Wiffle Ball
Warning

Mike and Kate spun around. Coach Caleb was standing behind them. "This area is for players only," he said. "You're not allowed here."

Mike and Kate took a step back.

"Oh, sorry!" Mike said. He pointed to Colin's team bag against the wall. "We were just helping Colin get his stuff."

Colin nodded. "It's okay, Coach," he said. "They're with me, and they're leaving soon to go to the parade, anyway."

Coach Caleb checked his watch. "Well, I've

got to get you guys ready for the parade as well."

As Coach Caleb turned to leave, Colin reached out and tugged on the sleeve of his shirt. "Um, one more thing, Coach," he said. "Would it be okay if Mike and Kate came to the parade with us? They could be like our team mascots or something!"

Coach Caleb studied Mike and Kate for a moment. "Hmm ... I don't know," he said. "They can't come on the float. But maybe they could walk alongside it."

Mike punched the air with his fist. "Woo-hoo!" he said. "We're going to be in a parade!" He gave Kate a high five.

The parade was huge. One team after another rode on the backs of flatbed tractor-trailer trucks. The teams sat on hay bales or stood and waved to the crowds as they drove down the main street of Williamsport. In between the team floats were marching bands, twirling troupes, tractors, and clowns. The crowds clapped for all the players but really went wild for the trucks giving out free bottles of PowerPunch, bags of potato chips, and candy bars.

"This is great!" Mike said. He waved to the crowds on both sides of the street as he and Kate walked alongside the Cooperstown float. Then he dug into a plastic bucket that he was carrying. He pulled out a handful of candy and threw it to little kids on the sides of the street. "I've just got to find a way to get one of the bottles of PowerPunch. All this sugar is making me thirsty!"

Kate waved and threw a handful of candy to the crowd. She pointed to two kids sitting on the curb and watching the parade. "Well, I'd like one of the bags of kettle corn they're eating," she said, and looked down at her bucket. "But I guess this will have to do for now!"

They passed TV cameras taking in the spectacle and a raised reviewing platform with two TV anchors narrating the parade.

At the end of the next block, the parade slowed down for a moment. Kate was waving at a group of little girls when she spotted someone near a telephone pole on a side street.

"Mike! Look at that!" Kate said as she pointed.

Mike followed Kate's direction. "Wow! It's him!" Mike said. Leaning against the telephone pole was a teenage boy wearing a neon green T-shirt.

"Do you think so?" Kate asked. "He does look like the kid that Zach told us about who ruined the tires on the bus!"

Mike nodded. "I think it is," he said. "Come on! Let's go talk to him! The float isn't going that fast. We can easily catch up. Give me your bucket."

Kate handed her candy over, and Mike ran to the side of the truck, near Colin. He handed Colin the two buckets. "Hold on to these for us," he said. "We'll be back in a minute!"

Before Colin could ask why, Mike jogged back to Kate. They ducked away from the float and crossed to the other side of the street. The telephone pole was set back from

the street, so Mike and Kate had to wind their way through the crowds of people sitting and standing along the curb.

But as they got closer, the boy in the neon green T-shirt spotted them. And he took off running! He ran down the side street, away from the crowd.

"Quick! We can catch him!" Kate said. She and Mike chased the boy. They ran down the side street, past parked cars and closed stores.

The boy darted left into an alleyway behind a convenience store.

"We got him now!" Mike said. He and Kate ran to the alley and turned into it.

But it was a dead end!

There was nothing in the alley except for an apartment building with three doors.

"Where'd he go?" Mike asked.

Kate studied the alley. She jangled the knobs on each of the doors. They were all locked.

"He must have ducked inside one of these apartments," Kate said. "It's like he disappeared!"

"That's too bad," Mike said. "I'll bet he's the one who ruined the tires on the bus! He was probably going to do something to the team when they went by on the float! Why else would he be waiting there like that?"

"I don't know," Kate said. "He sure took off in a hurry when he spotted us!"

Mike nodded. "He wouldn't have done that unless he had something to hide!"

Kate backed away from the doors. "But maybe he left a clue!" she said. "We need to get back to the parade, but we can look for clues on the way."

"Great idea!" Mike said. He scanned the ground as they walked.

Mike and Kate retraced their steps to the main street. They could hear the marching band in the distance. They zigzagged as they walked, looking for anything unusual on the ground.

"I don't see anything," Mike said as they approached the main street.

"Me neither," Kate said as she crossed in front of him. The telephone pole where they'd started was ahead of them.

"What about that?" Mike asked. An empty

potato chip bag fluttered against the side of a building.

Kate shook her head. She pointed to three little girls just beyond the building. Two of them were holding bags of chips. "Nice try!" she said. "But I don't think it's a clue."

"Maybe not," Mike said. "But what about that?"

Mike pointed to something white at the base of the telephone pole. He and Kate raced over.

Kate leaned down and picked up a white Wiffle ball. Written across its face in black marker were the words *Warning: Read my note!*

"Wow!" Mike said.

Warning Read my note!

Kate turned the ball around. A note was wedged into one of the holes in the ball. She pulled out the note and opened it.

Cooperstown—Don't bother trying!
The harder you try, the more you'll lose!
Today it was the tires.
Tomorrow it might be something bigger!

Mike looked from the telephone pole to the parade passing by. It was about fifteen feet away. "He must have been trying to throw the Wiffle ball onto the Cooperstown float!" he said. "That kid's out to get Cooperstown! We have to stop him!"

Kate nodded. As she scanned the ground around the telephone pole, a small green-and-gold object caught her eye. Kate leaned down and picked up a pin in the shape of a baseball diamond. The edges were gold, and the front was bright green. There was a picture of a dog standing on its hind legs and holding a rake. Underneath were the words *Super Dog.*

"Another clue!" she said. "This must be his, too."

Mike stared at it. "Hey, maybe we can use that to track him down," he said. "And I know the perfect place to start!"

A Surprising Loss

"There it is!" Mike said.

Mike pointed to a large tented area next to Lamade Stadium. It was ten o'clock the next morning, and he and Kate had just passed through the security entrance into the Little League grounds.

They walked past the warm-up field, where batters and pitchers were getting ready and reporters were doing interviews with teams. Fans watched from the sidewalk.

Kate checked the time. "We've got an hour

31

before Colin's team plays its first game," she said. "Let's get going!"

Mike and Kate made their way to a large red tent just outside the main stadium. When they stepped inside, they saw a bunch of picnic tables in the back corner.

"Over there!" Mike said. He and Kate headed for the pin-trading area. Small groups of kids and adults were clustered together. Some people had mats or felt rolled out in front of them, covered with multicolored pins. Others had large binders filled with pins mounted on thick pages.

Mike stepped up to the row of tables. He stuck his fingers in his mouth and gave a short whistle. Everyone turned to look at Mike.

"Hello!" Mike said. "I'm Mike Walsh, and this is Kate Hopkins. Sorry to interrupt, but I wanted to show you all something." He waved them over to the nearest picnic table.

The pin traders huddled around Mike and Kate. Mike took out the pin he and Kate had received yesterday for catching the dog. He held it up so everyone could see it.

"Ooh!" A gasp went out from the table.

"Wow! That's a founder's pin! Those are really hard to get!" said one kid.

Another kid held up his pin-trading binder. "I'll trade you ten of these pins for that one," he said. "You can pick any ten!"

"That's a super-rare pin," said an older girl sitting at the table. "They were only given out to really important people. I'd hold on to it, if I were you."

Mike slipped the pin back into his pocket. "Thanks!" he said. "I'm not going to trade this pin, but I'll give it away for free!"

A murmur went up from the pin traders. "For free?" asked a girl in a blue beret.

"I'll explain in a minute," Mike said. "But first I have another pin to show you." He held up the pin he and Kate had found near the telephone pole during the parade. Its gold edges sparkled in the light.

"Yesterday, we saw a teenager with a neon green T-shirt near a telephone pole on the main street," Mike said. "We think he dropped this, and we want to find him to talk about it."

The girl nearest Mike spoke up. "Oh, that's a Super Dog pin from last year," she said. "It's pretty rare, too. Only people who were on the Lamade Stadium grounds crew got one."

"Really?" Kate asked. "So maybe the kid who dropped it was on the grounds crew last year?"

"Well, maybe," the girl said. "But you can't be sure. He could have traded another pin for it."

Kate frowned. "Oh, right," she said. "Well, do any of you know a local kid who is on the grounds crew and wears a neon green T-shirt?"

Everyone shook their heads. "No," murmured one kid after another.

"We need to find the teenager with the neon green T-shirt," Mike said. "If anyone spots him, I'll give them this pin for *free!*" He held out the founder's pin, and everyone's eyes opened wide.

"Cool!" said the girl with the blue beret.

"Wow, great!" said a boy in the back.

Mike and Kate left the pin-trading area and walked outside the tent. The bright sunshine was making the day warm.

"We should find a way to investigate the grounds crew," Kate said.

"Good idea, but we don't really have enough time before Colin's game," Mike said.

Kate tapped Mike on the shoulder. "Actually, we do have time—we can do both at the same time!" she said. "What if we go watch Colin's game and then also watch the grounds crew for anyone suspicious!"

Mike smiled. "That sounds like a plan," he said.

They wound their way through the crowds to the side entrance to Lamade Stadium. They walked up a long path onto the sidewalk that ringed the stadium. The thousands of seats were mostly filled. Clustered above the seats behind home plate were reporters and TV cameras. Kate spotted her mom in the press area and waved. Mrs. Hopkins waved back and smiled.

"Wow! This stadium is huge," Mike said. "I wish we could play a game here. It would be like playing at a real major-league park!"

"Let's find some seats," Kate said.

As they rounded the curve behind home plate, Kate spotted a man and his son getting up near the dugout. "Quick, over there!" Kate said. She and Mike darted down the aisle just as the pair walked away.

"Score!" Mike said as he slipped down in

the seat. He gave Kate a high five. "These are great!"

"And just as the game is about to start!" Kate said.

But it didn't. The start time for the game came and went. The coaches walked out onto the field to meet with the umpire. The umpire kept checking his watch and finally pointed to it. Coach Caleb looked upset.

"Welcome to Lamade Stadium," a deep-voiced announcer said over the loudspeaker. "We're having some technical difficulties. Please be patient while we try to fix them. The game should be starting shortly."

Mike turned to Kate. "I wonder what's going on," he said. "This doesn't seem good."

"No, it doesn't," Kate said.

"Hey, look," Mike said. "What's Colin doing over there?"

He pointed to the other side of home plate. Colin had left the dugout and was standing at the railing near the seats. He seemed to be scanning the crowd.

"Come on. We'd better go check that out," Kate said.

Kate and Mike ran over to the foul ball net near Colin.

"Colin! What's up?" Mike asked as they skidded to a halt.

"Oh, great!" Colin said. "I was looking for you. We need your help."

"What do you mean?" Mike asked. "I know I've got a good swing, but I don't think I'm allowed to bat."

Colin shook his head. "We don't need your baseball skills," he said. "We need your detective skills. Someone stole all our equipment bags!"

A White Line

"A thief is trying to sabotage our team!" Colin said. "We can't start the game until our bags are found. Nobody has their gloves or helmets or bats! If we don't find them in fifteen minutes, we'll have to forfeit the game!"

"Oh no!" Kate said. "When did you have them last?"

"About half an hour ago," Colin said. "We left the Grove with the bags and came down to the stadium. Zach told us to pile them next to the stadium entrance while we waited for the

Mexico versus Japan game to finish. We all walked over to the outfield grass and watched the end of the game. When we came back, our bags were gone!"

"We'll help," Mike said. "Kate and I can look for the bags."

Colin's face broke into a big smile. "That'd be great," he said. "We really need your help. Coach Caleb got the security team to look for

them, but I'm not sure they're going to find them in time!"

"We're on it!" Kate said. "Come on, Mike. Let's start looking for clues near the stadium entrance."

Mike and Kate brushed past the fans still streaming into the stadium. They wound down the long entrance ramp and emerged back into the sunshine.

The outside area was filled with fans and teams in bright orange and green uniforms on their way to the second stadium. Hickory-scented smoke rose from a large barbecue food stand. And there were lines of people waiting to try out their baseball skills in the Fun Zone area.

Mike pointed to the outside corner of the stadium near the entrance. "They must have piled their bags there," he said. "Let's take a closer look."

Mike and Kate ran over to the corner of the stadium. The red brick of the stadium wall rose up from the dark blacktop.

Kate scanned the area. "This whole place is paved, so we can't search for footprints," she said. "And I don't see any trace of the bags. Maybe someone saw the thief take them?"

Kate looked at the stores and stands across from the stadium. "What about that girl at the cotton-candy stand?" she asked. "Let's ask her."

They ran across to the food stand. A teen-age girl was running the register and selling bags of bright blue and pink cotton candy. Two people were in line. When it was Kate's turn, she stepped up to the counter and asked the girl if she had noticed anyone taking the team's bags.

The girl looked across the stadium and shook her head. "I've been so busy all morning, I wasn't really looking up that much," she said. The girl thought for a moment. "The only thing I can remember noticing was one of the TV reporters driving an ATV earlier this morning. But I didn't see any baseball bags on it."

"Okay, thanks for the help," Mike said. He and Kate headed back across to the stadium.

"That's not a very strong lead," Mike said. "And we don't have much time. Let's start at the spot where the bags were and spread out to look for clues."

Kate nodded. She and Mike started scanning the blacktop near the stadium again.

A moment later, Mike leaned down. "Hey, look at this," he called out.

Kate ran over. Mike knelt and pointed to something white on the ground. "A trail!" he said.

A faint trail of white powder ran along the side of the building. It was hard to see unless you knew to look for it.

"Let's follow it!" Mike said. He stood up and followed the trail as it snaked along the outside of the stadium, past a few maintenance doors and a closed ticket area. The white line seemed to grow fainter in some places.

"Where'd it go?" Kate asked. The line stopped in the middle of one of the wide garage doors on the side of the stadium, beneath the stands. She walked farther along the building but didn't see any trace of the white line.

Mike studied the stadium and the garage door. "Well, either it stopped for some reason," he said, "or it goes under this door!"

Kate nodded. "It definitely doesn't go any farther that way," she said. "So I think we've only got one choice. Let's look inside. There's no sign saying we can't. Give me a hand."

Kate reached down and grabbed the

handle of the garage door. Mike helped her give the handle a tug. The door rumbled and rolled up.

Sunlight shot into a cavernous space filled with equipment and supplies for field maintenance. Mike and Kate spotted rakes, shovels, buckets, hoses, and piles of line chalk and quick-drying materials for the field.

Mike scanned the floor for the white line. He spotted it just inside the door. He pointed it out to Kate, and they followed it to an ATV parked in the back corner.

The bed of the ATV was covered with a big tarp.

Kate lifted the corner of the tarp a little to peek underneath.

"Aha!" she said.

"What? Did you find the bags?" Mike asked.

"No," Kate said. "But here's where the white line came from!"

Mike took a look.

An empty bag of line chalk lay on the edge of the cart. The bottom of the bag, hanging over the edge of the cart, was ripped.

"The white line came from this bag of chalk," Mike said. "It must have been leaking out as the ATV drove in here."

Kate nodded. She leaned forward and pulled back the tarp even more.

On the back of the ATV was a huge pile of baseball backpacks! They all had *Cooperstown* stitched on their side in white letters.

"We found them!" Mike said.

"And just in time!" Kate said. She grabbed two bags. "Come on, get a couple and we'll take them to the team!"

Mike and Kate raced back around the

stadium and up the walkway to the fence near the Cooperstown dugout.

"Colin! Colin!" Kate called.

A moment later, Colin came out of the dugout and ran over to Mike and Kate.

"Look what we found!" Mike said. He held up a Cooperstown baseball backpack with bats sticking up on the sides and a glove dangling from the back.

"You did it!" Colin shouted. "Woo-hoo!" He let out a loud whistle. "This is great. Do you have the rest of them?"

Kate nodded. "They're all on the other side of the stadium in the grounds equipment room," she said.

"Thanks, guys!" Colin said. "I'll tell Coach, and we'll get them! You've saved the day!"

The Close One

Mike and Kate slid down into their seats. On the other side of the netting, Colin and the Cooperstown team were getting ready for the game.

"That proves it!" Kate said. "We have to investigate the grounds crew and find the boy in the neon green T-shirt."

Mike nodded. He pointed to three men running around the infield with rakes and a chalk-line machine. "It's not them. They're all too old," he said. "After the game let's see if we can find the grounds crew manager and interview him."

The three men on the grounds crew ran off the field, and the loudspeakers crackled, "Welcome to the first game of the series!"

The crowd roared to life. Fans clapped and whistled.

After the national anthem played, a player from the Cooperstown Mid-Atlantic team and one from the New England team jogged out to the infield with their coaches. They took turns reciting the Little League Pledge.

As soon as they finished, the kids and coaches ran back to their dugouts. The loud-speaker crackled again, and the announcer introduced the players on each team. When a player's name was called, they ran out and lined up on the field.

"Look at those TV cameras," Mike said.

He pointed to men walking around on the field with big TV cameras, getting close-ups of the players waving. "It would be so cool to be playing in the game and to be on national TV!"

When the introductions were done, the announcer continued. "We have one more thing to do before the game starts. We'd like to ask all the players and coaches to join Dugout, our Little League mascot, and dance to the song 'Cotton-Eyed Joe'!"

The air was filled with the sound of wailing fiddles, singing banjos, and thumping drums as the country song streamed out over the field. Dugout, who looked like a cross between a chipmunk and a beaver, led players and coaches in a comical line dance. The crowd clapped along with the song, and a few fans yelled "Yee-haw!" and pretended to swing a lasso over their heads.

As the last few fiddle sounds floated away, the players and coaches bowed and ran back to their dugouts.

"And now it's time for baseball!" the announcer called out. "Plaaaaaay ball!"

The New England team from West Newton, Massachusetts, was up first. Colin's Mid-Atlantic team from Cooperstown, New York, took the field.

The West Newton team came out swinging.

Their first two batters got hits. But then Cooperstown shut them down and struck out the next three batters. The teams switched places, and Cooperstown's Logan Fogg stepped up to the plate. On the second pitch, he launched the ball into the sky!

The West Newton fielders raced for it, but it was no use. It was a home run! Fogg circled the bases as the Cooperstown fans exploded in cheers. The score was 1–0, Cooperstown!

But the inning ended without any more runs. Cooperstown's Nicole Brooks took the mound for the second inning and threw a one-two-three inning, with three outs for the first three batters. Over the next two innings, Cooperstown scored two more runs. West Newton only got one. But in the top of the fourth inning, Brooks melted down. After

she allowed one person on base after another, West Newton's Scott Kelly hit an inside-the-park grand slam, putting West Newton ahead by two runs!

Coach Caleb from Cooperstown pulled Brooks, but the damage was done. The team kept making mistakes. On a simple play in the fifth inning, Colin threw from second to first, but the ball sailed over the head of the first baseman and West Newton scored again.

In the sixth and final inning, Cooperstown almost found their groove when Colin hit a double with one out. The next two batters singled, and Colin scored. The fourth batter struck out, but the fifth banged a single to load the bases. A grand slam would put Cooperstown ahead!

"Come on, Cooperstown!" Kate yelled. The

Cooperstown fans clapped and cheered. The noise was deafening!

Ryan Poole stepped to the plate. He watched two balls go by but swung at the third pitch—a fastball! The ball popped high up in the air as the runners advanced. Poole ran for first, but the West Newton catcher ripped off his mask and stepped forward. The ball flew over home plate, peaked, and fell back down.

PLOP!

Straight into the catcher's glove. It was an out! No one scored.

The game was over. Cooperstown lost!

Mike and Kate couldn't believe it. The West Newton players ran screaming toward their pitcher and bounced around in a group at the pitcher's mound.

The Cooperstown team slunk off the field.

Breaking News

"Oh no! Colin's team lost!" Kate said. "They're out of the tournament! It's all because someone stole their bags!"

Mike shook his head. "No, it's okay," he said. "The series is double elimination. That means teams keep playing until they lose twice." He pointed to the schedule. "Look at the chart. Even though they lost, they'll play again tomorrow!"

Out on the field, Coach Caleb gathered the Cooperstown players in right field. They knelt in a circle around him while he spoke.

Kate leaned forward. She nudged Mike. "Okay, great," she said. "Then we need to watch the grounds crew. We still have a job to do!"

Mike stood and followed the grounds-keepers as they jogged out to the infield with rakes. "It looks like the same three that we saw before the game," he said. "I don't see a teenager anywhere."

Kate nodded. The groundskeepers cleaned up home plate and the pitcher's mound and smoothed the base paths. A few minutes later they left the field.

Coach Caleb finished his talk. The Cooperstown team headed for the dugout to pick up their stuff.

"Time to go," Mike said. He and Kate walked up the aisle and out of the stadium.

It was still a sunny day, and Lamade Stadium felt light with excitement. Mike and Kate headed over to the big staircase that rose up to the sidewalk in front of the Grove. When they reached the top, they stepped off to the side. A group of kids was already waiting there with autograph books and baseball gloves.

"Good game!" said one fan after another as West Newton lined up in front of the Grove security gate.

Kate sighed. "I feel bad for Colin's team," she said. "It's unfair that someone messed them up by stealing their bags before the game."

Mike nodded. "There they are!" he said. Colin's team had just started up the stairs. By the time they reached the top, Mike and Kate were the only fans waiting for them.

"Good game!" Mike said as Coach Caleb walked by.

"Colin! Nice hit!" Kate said. "Sorry you lost!"

Colin stopped and dropped his backpack to the ground. "It's okay. We tried, but the other team played better," he said. "We're going to shake it off and come out swinging tomorrow. It's not over until it's over!"

"I know it feels bad for you, but it's good for us!" said a deep voice from behind them.

Mike, Kate, and Colin turned. It was Matt the TV reporter, with a microphone and a camera guy behind him.

"I'm sorry you lost, guys, but our audience loves a tough fight!" he said. "We thought you were going to sail through and clobber your opponents, but this is even better for our fans at home. They love the competition!"

He held the microphone in front of Colin's face. "Do you have anything to say to the team you're playing tomorrow?" he asked.

Colin smiled. "Sure, I just have one thing I'd like to say," he said. "Good luck! May the best team win!"

Matt smiled. "Well, there you have it," he said. "I expect we'll have a huge audience for that game!" He turned to the camera. "Make sure to join us tomorrow when we find out if our Cooperstown heroes are going home win-ners or losers!"

Colin shook his head. "We're going home winners," he said. "No matter what our record is!"

A loud whistle pierced the air. Coach Caleb gestured his team toward the security gate. Colin picked up his backpack and started for the Grove. He looked over his shoulder at Mike and Kate. "See you later!" he said.

Mike and Kate waved, and then Kate turned to Mike. "Let's go!" she said. "We've got to check things out. We can't let anything else happen to Colin's team before tomorrow's game!"

They bounded back down the stairs and around the outside of Lamade Stadium. They stopped short when they reached the equipment room where they had found the missing backpacks. The garage door was open, and two men were standing in the far corner talking.

Kate knocked on the frame of the door. "Hello," she said.

The two men turned. "Can I help you?" said the man on the left. He was wearing a red, white, and blue baseball cap and a white T-shirt.

"Um, yes," Mike said. He and Kate walked over to where the two men were standing. He reached into his pocket and held out the Super Dog pin. "Do you recognize this pin?"

"Oh, sure," the man in the cap said. "Everyone on the grounds crew got one of those last year. Why?"

"Because we're trying to find the boy who lost this one," Kate said. "We were wondering

if he was on the grounds crew last year."

"Oh, okay," the man said. "What's his name?"

Mike and Kate looked at each other. "We don't know, actually," Mike said. "He's a teenager. He's thin. And when we saw him, he was wearing a neon green T-shirt."

"Hmm," said the second man. "We only have about ten people on the grounds crew, and only the adults are on it year after year.

We have a new group of teenagers helping out this year."

"I don't remember whether any of the kids on the crew last year had green shirts," the first man said. "I think some of the kids on the crew last year were Donald, Sammy, Graham, and Alicia. But I don't know if that helps."

Kate nodded. "Thanks, it might," she said. "Our friend Colin is on the Cooperstown team. And we are trying to figure out how their baseball backpacks ended up in here, on that ATV in the corner."

Both men shook their heads. "We don't know, either," the first man said. "We're pretty busy before the games, so there's a lot that goes on that we don't see."

"Do you know if anyone drove that ATV this morning?" Mike asked.

"Well, I did," the first man said. "I had to take a bunch of line chalk to the field. But someone else on the staff might have used it, too. We often just leave these out there, along the side of the stadium, in case we need to use them."

The second man raised a finger. "Oh yeah," he said. "I know someone else who asked to use the ATV this morning. Matt the TV reporter needed to move camera equipment or something."

Mike looked at Kate and raised his eyebrows.

"Thanks," Kate said. "That's helpful."

The first man tipped his hat to Mike and Kate. "You're welcome," he said. "Glad we could help."

Mike and Kate walked back outside and stopped when they were out of earshot.

"Are you thinking what I'm thinking?" Kate asked.

Mike nodded. "Yup!" he said. "Our TV reporter friend could have been the one who stole the bags!"

A Mysterious Boss

"Exactly!" Kate said. "He was in the right place at the right time. And he has a motive! He's trying to sabotage the Cooperstown team to get more viewers for his TV show!"

"We've got to stop him!" Mike said.

Kate nodded. She checked the time. "The next game hasn't started yet," she said. "So he may be at the All-Star Sports Network booth on the other side of the stadium. I saw them doing a broadcast from there earlier."

Mike and Kate ran along the outside of

Lamade Stadium to a big booth near the Fun Zone area. Large TV cameras stood facing the booth.

"That's him!" Kate said as they entered the booth. Matt was sitting behind a big table, with another reporter next to him. They were both holding microphones and talking to the cameras.

"Well, at least now we know where he is," Mike said. "Let's wait here and follow him when he's done."

"Good idea," Kate said. They watched the reporters talk. But after a few minutes, Mike got bored and started looking around. He noticed the hickory smoke rising from the barbecue stand.

"Mmm! That barbecue sure smells good," Mike said. "It doesn't look like Matt's going anywhere soon. Maybe we should head over there and get some extra energy for all this detective work. I could go for a pulled-pork sandwich and a PowerPunch!"

"Food's not a bad idea," Kate said. "But one of us should stay here and keep an eye on Matt."

Mike raised his hand. "I'll go!" he said as he sniffed the air a few more times. "I'll get the food and be back faster than a cardboard sled going down that hill!"

Kate stared at Mike. "What did you say?" she asked.

Mike bounced up and down and pretended to sprint. "I'll go faster than the sleds we used yesterday! Why, you want me to go faster?"

Kate glanced back at Matt. He was still talking into his microphone and looking at the camera.

"We have a problem. Matt can't be the one

interfering with Colin's team," Kate said. "He wasn't at the rest stop yesterday, so he couldn't have destroyed the tires on the bus."

"How do we know he wasn't there?" Mike asked.

"Because I almost slid into him yesterday with the cardboard sleds, remember?" Kate said. "He was on the hill with us at the same time the bus was at the rest stop. It's not him!"

Mike looked from Kate to the TV reporter and back. He nodded. Then he clicked his fingers. "Unless . . . ," he said.

Kate leaned forward. "Unless what?" she asked.

"Unless he *hired* someone else to do it for him!" Mike said. "What if he hired someone at the rest stop to slit the tires and slow the team down?"

"And then he stole the bags himself today!"

Kate said. She nodded. "You're right. It *might* be him!"

Before Mike or Kate could decide what to do next, they heard a rustling noise behind them.

Mike and Kate turned around. A boy with an orange baseball cap was running straight at them! He skidded to a halt.

"I've been looking all over for you two!" the boy said. "I found him!"

"You found Matt the TV reporter?" Mike

asked. "We already know where he is! He's right over there." He pointed to the broadcast booth.

"No!" said the boy. "I found the kid with the neon green T-shirt that you were looking for! You said you'd give us your founder's pin if we found him, and I did!"

"Really?" Kate asked. "Where is he?"

The boy held out his hand. "Not so fast," he said. "Where's the founder's pin?"

Kate glanced at Mike. "He has it in his pocket," she said. "But we can't give it to you until we actually *see* the kid in the neon green T-shirt."

The boy thought for a moment and nodded. "Okay, deal," he said. "Follow me!"

The boy led them around the outside of Lamade Stadium. They passed the main gift shop, the pin-trading tent, a large food court, and the restrooms. On the far side of the stadium the boy followed the sidewalk leading to the giant scoreboard on the hill behind the outfield.

"Where's he taking us?" Kate whispered to Mike.

But just before passing the edge of the stadium, the boy stopped. He waited for Mike and Kate to catch up and then pointed across the sidewalk to a green-and-yellow lemonade stand.

"The kid you're looking for is right there!" the boy said.

He was right!

The boy who Mike and Kate had chased at the parade was working at the lemonade stand. In the back of the stand, an older man wearing a green shirt was preparing big glasses of freshly squeezed lemonade. Up at the front of the stand a girl was taking orders and handing customers drinks. The boy who Mike and Kate were looking for was restocking cups and getting lemons for the older man. And he was wearing the neon green T-shirt!

"That's him, all right," Mike said.

Kate nodded. "That's *definitely* the kid we saw at the parade!"

The boy who led them there held out his hand. "Okay, great!" he said. "I think I delivered the goods. Now it's your turn."

Mike glanced at the boy's outstretched hand. He dug into his pocket and pulled out the founder's pin. He held it up for Kate to see. She nodded. Mike took one last look at it and dropped it into the boy's hand.

"Thanks for helping us!" he said. "Can you let the rest of the pin traders know that we found our man?"

The boy smiled. "Oh, you know I will," he said. "They're going to know big-time because now I've got one of the best pins ever to show off! See you later!"

He put the pin in his pocket and raced toward the pin-trading tent.

"We've got him!" Kate said as she and Mike turned back to face the lemonade stand.

"Yes, but how do we *get* him?" Mike asked. "He's working!"

"Look!" Kate said. "He's going outside to get more supplies!" The boy in the green shirt exited a door and walked to the side of the stand. There were big boxes of cups, straws, and lemons. He picked up two stacks of cups and went back inside.

"Great!" Mike said. "We can wait over there and nab him when he comes out for more supplies!"

Mike and Kate walked around to the back of the stand and knelt behind the boxes of cups. It took a while for the boy to come outside again, but when he finally did, Mike and Kate stepped out from behind the boxes.

"Hey, you were in the parade! What are you doing back here?" the boy said. "Are you stealing our food?"

"No, but our friend Colin is on the Cooperstown team, and we've got a question for you," Kate said. "We want to know why you slit the tires of their bus!"

The boy tilted his head and stared at Kate. "What do you mean? I didn't slit the tires of any bus."

"Then why'd you run away at the parade?" Mike asked.

"Because you were chasing me!" the boy said. "I didn't know what you wanted!"

Mike looked at Kate. The conversation wasn't going the way they'd thought it would.

Kate took a chance. "What about the backpacks?" she said. "Did you move the Cooperstown backpacks?"

The boy paused. He scratched the side of his head and looked at the ground.

"Um, yeah," he said.

Mike's eyes opened wide. "You did?" he said. "How?"

"I waited for the team to drop their backpacks, and then I loaded them onto the ATV and drove them into the equipment room," the boy said. "I worked on the grounds crew last year and used to drive the ATV all the time."

"But why'd you do it?" Kate asked.

The boy shrugged. "Because someone paid me to."

"Who?" Kate asked. "Who paid you to move Cooperstown's backpacks?"

"It's not really a secret," the boy said. "It was Coach Caleb from the Cooperstown team."

Big Daddy Hacks

"What?" Mike said. "You're kidding! Coach Caleb?"

The boy shook his head. "I'm not kidding," he said. "Coach Caleb told me he wanted to toughen up his team and make them take more responsibility. It's not a big deal. They got their backpacks before the game."

"Yes! Because *we* found them!" Kate said. "When did Coach Caleb hire you? He just arrived with the team yesterday! Why were you at the parade?"

"I do a lot of work around Williamsport," the boy said. He pulled out his phone. "I use an app on my phone. People post jobs they want done and how much they'll pay, and I do them!" He woke up his phone and pulled up the job app. The boy scrolled through some listings and pointed to one.

Wanted: Teenager to help teach my team a lesson in Williamsport. —Coach Caleb, Cooperstown

"Once I took the job, Coach Caleb said I needed to do two things. The first was to watch the parade with a neon green T-shirt on and throw a Wiffle ball with a message in it. The second was to hide the baseball backpacks of the Cooperstown team before their first game," the boy said. "He said it was all to teach them a lesson about responsibility. He seemed happy. The money got credited to my account yesterday."

"So you talked to Coach Caleb?" Kate asked.

"Ah, no," the boy said. "We did this over email." The boy glanced at the lemonade stand. "Listen, I've got to get back to work. Do you need anything else?"

Mike shrugged. "I guess not," he said. He looked at Kate. "Do we have any more questions?"

Kate shook her head. "No," she said. "I don't know what we're looking for now."

Mike reached into his pocket and pulled something out. "Here," he said. "I think this is yours, and you should probably have it back." He held out the Super Dog pin that he and Kate had found near the telephone pole.

"Oh, wow!" the boy said. He reached out

and took the pin. "Thanks! I lost this the other day and couldn't find it anywhere." He smiled at Mike and Kate. "Thanks. I've really got to get back to work." He grabbed two more stacks of cups and scooted back into the stand.

Mike kicked at the dirt with his sneaker. "Well, I guess we can rule out Matt the TV reporter," he said.

"Yup," Kate said. "Coach Caleb! It's hard to believe that Coach Caleb would do it, but I guess we have the evidence. He must have slit the tires on the bus, too. But that's not a good way to teach a lesson."

"We need to chase him down now," Mike said. "Before he does something else to the team."

"We can't!" Kate said. "They're in the Grove for the rest of the day."

"Then we need to do it first thing tomorrow

morning!" Mike said. "We'll wait for the team at the gate and have a little talk with Coach Caleb."

"Good idea!" Kate said.

Mike nodded. He spotted a big map on the wall of the stadium. "And I've got another good idea," he said. "Follow me!"

Mike led Kate over to the large map. "As long as we have extra time, we should go here." He pointed on the map to a building that was just outside the front gates.

"The World of Little League Museum?" Kate asked. "Okay, cool!"

Kate followed as Mike ran past the main entrance gates to the museum next door. He pulled the door open just as Kate skidded to a halt.

The museum was larger than it looked from the outside. It was filled with exhibits about the history of Little League and the Little League World Series. It had lots of old gloves, baseballs, rule books, and other baseball equipment from the early days of the league.

It also had cool exhibits like a compressed-air cannon that was used to shoot baseballs at baseball helmets to test them. And one where visitors could put on 3-D glasses and pretend to be a catcher. Mike really liked the one that timed how fast he ran to first base.

Near the end of the exhibits was one that showed famous events in the Little League World Series over the years. There were movies of early World Series games and descriptions of other important games. Kate was reading them when something caught her eye.

"Hey, Mike, come here!" she said.

Mike ran over from the shortstop exhibit.

"Here's an article that talks about the last time the Cooperstown team made it to the series, ten years ago, and set the record for a comeback," she said. "And look, there's a big feature on Zach. It tells all about the Big Daddy Hacks that he was famous for taking at the plate. He hit three home runs that game and drove in seven runs!"

Mike stared at a blown-up picture of Zach holding his bat and smiling in front of Lamade Stadium. TV cameras and reporters were surrounding him.

Mike studied the picture. "Wow! That's so cool to be in a museum!" he said. "I hope I can be that important someday."

Kate nodded. "That would be awesome," she said.

They followed the hallway to the next room.

"Oh, I guess that's it," Mike said as they turned a corner. Ahead was the exit to the gift shop. He was just about to go through the turnstile when Kate called out.

"Wait!" she said. "Come back here for a minute."

Mike ran back to the exhibit of famous Little League World Series moments. Kate pointed to the article on the Cooperstown team again.

"This article gave me an idea," she said. "What if it's not Coach Caleb who is doing everything? What if it's really his son, *Zach*?"

The Old Phone Trick

"Zach?" Mike asked.

"Yes!" she said. "It all fits together! He was on the bus at the rest stop, so he could have cut the tires and made up the story about the kid with the neon green T-shirt. And he could have used that phone app to hire the kid to move the team's equipment! He just called himself Coach Caleb so there would be an explanation for why he wanted the bags moved. Zach was impersonating his father. The boy with the neon green T-shirt would have no idea since it was all done over email and through the app!"

"But why Zach?" Mike asked.

Kate tapped on the glass case that held the articles on display. "Because of this!" she said. "Zach doesn't want this year's Cooperstown team to do better than his team did ten years ago! He's probably jealous. He wants

to be the most famous baseball player from Cooperstown!"

"So Zach hired the kid with the neon green T-shirt to hang out near the parade where the kids on the float would see him and he'd throw the threatening message to them," Mike said. "He probably told him to wear a neon green T-shirt to match up with his story about the teenager cutting the bus tires. He worked it all out in advance!"

"So Coach Caleb has nothing to do with this," Kate said. "We need to stop *Zach*! One more loss and Cooperstown is finished."

"But we can't get into the Grove," Mike said. "How can we stop him?"

Kate thought for a moment. "I have an idea!" she said. "If we can find a thrift store tonight, I know how we can catch him tomorrow morning."

It was only ten o'clock when Mike and Kate passed through the security check the next day, but the sun was bright, and it was already hot out.

"You think this will work?" Mike asked Kate as they walked up the main path to Lamade Stadium.

"It *has* to," Kate said. "We've only got one chance before Cooperstown plays this afternoon! Do you have the phone?"

Mike pulled a phone out of his pocket enough for Kate to see it. "Yup," he said. "I've got it ready! I'm glad we were able to find one at the thrift store yesterday. This is the kind of thing I'm good at!"

Kate smiled. "I know," she said. "That's why I'm letting you handle it!"

Mike and Kate hurried along the main path to Lamade Stadium but didn't enter it. Instead, they wound their way up the stairs leading to the Grove. A minute later they reached the top. The gates to the Grove were open, but three employees sat at tables checking identification and keeping fans out.

"Now we wait," Kate said. She and Mike leaned against a nearby railing and watched fans stream into the stadium below them. A small group of kids was nearby with pens and pads ready, waiting to ask the players for autographs.

A few minutes later, the team from Mexico walked through the gate. They high-fived fans, and a few of the players signed autographs. A couple of families took pictures with their players.

"*¡Buena suerte!*" Kate called as they headed down the stairs to the fields. "Good luck!"

Before long, Colin's team walked through the gate. Coach Caleb was in the lead. The players were all dressed in their uniforms and lugging their baseball backpacks. Even though they didn't have a game until later that afternoon, they had a practice scheduled for that morning on the lower practice fields.

"There's Colin!" Kate said.

"And there's Zach!" Mike said. "He's at the gate. Let's move around to the back, near him."

Before heading down the stairs, Coach Caleb stopped the group and counted the players. "Good!" he called. "We have everyone here. Today's a big day, and we're going to do great. We're here to play our best! What do we say?"

The team erupted in a cheer:

Hey, hey!

Get out of our way!

Today is the day

We put you away!

"That's it!" Coach Caleb yelled. "And remember—they say *play ball* for a reason! It's supposed to be fun!"

"Let's do it!" called a player from the back.

"We got this one!" said another.

Coach Caleb turned and started to lead the team down the stairs to the practice fields. As he did, Mike and Kate moved closer to Zach. Zach was at the back of the group of players, waiting to follow Coach Caleb.

"Hey, Zach!" Mike said. "We saw your picture in the museum yesterday! It was really cool!"

Zach's face lit up. "Thanks! It's great to be back here to relive all those great memories from our big game."

"Hey, Zach, do you know what time it is?" Mike asked. "I think I'm supposed to call my mother now."

Zach pulled out his phone. "It's ten-thirty," he said.

"Thanks," Mike said. "Time to call Mom!"

Mike made a big show of pulling a phone out of his pocket. But as the phone cleared the top of his pants pocket, he flicked his hand slightly.

"Oh no!" Mike called out. The phone flew through the air and smashed onto the black-top. Slivers of glass shone in the sun, and small plastic parts flew into the grass.

"Mike!" Kate said. "You're the clumsiest person I know!"

"My phone!" Mike said. He jumped over to pick up the phone, but his front foot landed directly on it. It made a loud crunching sound.

"I can't believe you did that!" Kate said.

Mike moved his foot and knelt. He picked up the mangled phone and then looked at Zach.

"Um, hey, Zach, can I borrow your phone to call my mother?" Mike asked. "I promise I'll be careful."

Zach thought for a moment. "Sure, but maybe just step over there on the grass while you're using it in case you drop it," he said. He walked up to Mike, unlocked his phone, and handed it to him.

As Mike swiped and poked at the phone's touchscreen, Kate walked over near Zach.

"Zach, I have a question about that big game you were in ten years ago," Kate said. "It sounds like one of the reasons you won was because of your hitting style. Can you tell me how you did it?"

Zach turned to Kate. "That's right, my Big

Daddy Hacks were the reason we were able to come back from so far behind," he said. "But I'm sorry, it's really a secret. I don't like to share it with anyone. Nothing personal!"

Kate nodded. "That's too bad," she said. "It seemed like it might help the team win the next game if you could teach them."

Zach shook his head. "They've been asking me all season for the secret," he said. "But I don't give Big Daddy Hack lessons to anyone. It's my secret."

Over on the grass, Mike cleared his throat. "Hey, Zach! You do seem to be teaching the team some other types of lessons," he said. "I think the real Coach Caleb will be very interested in them."

Zach looked at Mike. Mike raised his hand and held Zach's phone so the screen was facing out.

On the screen was the app that the boy with the green shirt had shown them yesterday. And at the top was the message that the boy had pulled up for Mike and Kate:

Wanted: Teenager to help teach my team a lesson in Williamsport. —Coach Caleb, Cooperstown

"We know you're impersonating Coach Caleb," Kate said. "And now we can prove it. And we also know you're trying to sabotage the Cooperstown team so they don't do better than your team did."

Mike took out his real phone and snapped a picture of the message on Zach's phone for proof. "When your dad finds out what you've been doing," he said, "I have a feeling your time with the team will be over!"

It's About Playing, Not Winning

Zach leaned against the fence. "How did you find out?" he asked.

"We talked with the boy you hired to move the bags and throw the Wiffle ball at the parade," Kate said. "He showed us this message, and we thought it came from your dad until we saw your picture in the museum yesterday. That's when we realized it was you."

"We also know you cut the bus tires!" Mike said. "You're the only one who witnessed it.

You made up the story about the kid with the neon green shirt, and then you hired someone to make the team think someone was after them!"

"Someone *was* after them," Kate said. "But it was you!"

Mike handed Zach's phone back.

"This is the end of the line for your tricks, Zach," Mike said.

Zach straightened up. "But this team is so good!" he said as he waved his arms. "They might win the whole tournament! If they do, no one will remember me or my game ten years ago!" Zach tapped his chest. "I was just trying to toughen them up and scare them a little. I wasn't going to hurt anyone, but I didn't want them to win the series!"

Kate shook her head. "But, Zach, that's

not the way to get people to remember you! People will remember you if you help them, not hurt them!" she said.

Zach shrugged. "I don't know," he said.

Kate pointed at Lamade Stadium. "You still have an amazing opportunity to help the Cooperstown team win!" she said. "You could be part of the reason they win it all. Wouldn't that feel better than trying to mess up their chances?"

Zach looked at Kate. "What do you mean? What can I do to help the team?" he asked in a soft voice.

"No one else has the Big Daddy Hacks way of hitting a baseball!" Kate said. She motioned toward the practice fields below the stadium. "It's not too late for you to teach it to the players on the team! They're down there practicing right now."

Zach scuffed the blacktop with his sneaker. He jammed his hands into his pockets and shook his head. "It's too late," he said. "I've already messed up the team's chances, and my dad will never forgive me."

"It's not too late! The team still needs you," Mike said. "And you don't know what your dad will say until you tell him what you've done."

"And what you're going to do!" Kate added. "Come on, now's the time!"

Zach glanced from Kate to Mike. He stood up straight, took his hands out of his pockets, and nodded. "That's a good idea!" he said. "I'm going to do the right thing!"

Mike and Kate smiled. They gave Zach a fist bump. "Let's do it!" Kate said.

The three ran down the stairs, taking two steps at time. Zach led the race past Lamade

Stadium and down to the lower fields, where the teams were practicing.

Zach ran over to his dad. Mike and Kate watched as Zach explained everything to him. When Zach was done, Coach Caleb took off his baseball hat and scratched his head. He looked at the players running drills on the field and then back to Zach. After a moment, Coach Caleb leaned over and gave Zach a hug!

Mike and Kate high-fived. "I think that's a good sign," Kate said.

Coach Caleb called the Cooperstown team to huddle. The kids ran over and listened to Coach Caleb, and then Zach got in front of them and talked for a few minutes. When he was done, he looked down at the ground. The team was silent for a moment, and then Coach Caleb asked a question. A moment later, the

team erupted in cheers and threw their hats in the air.

"Big Daddy Hacks for everyone!" yelled one player.

Everyone on the team popped up and high-fived Zach! As soon as they finished, Zach led the first group of players to the batting cages and started teaching them his special hitting technique.

"I guess they forgave him," Mike said.

Kate nodded. "I think so," she said. "Let's hope Zach can help them win their game this afternoon!"

When the game between Cooperstown and the team from Chula Vista, California, started that afternoon at three o'clock, it wasn't hard to tell whether Zach's help had made a difference.

The Cooperstown team got one hit after another. After three innings, Cooperstown was ahead by six! Three of the Cooperstown players, including Colin, had hit home runs!

And it didn't stop there. Even though Chula Vista rallied in the fifth inning to get three runs, Cooperstown held them off and knocked in two runs in the second half of the fifth inning.

"Just one more inning!" Kate said. She and Mike were watching the game from a front-row seat they had scored an hour before the game started. "Chula Vista will have to get five runs to send the game into extra innings. And that's not easy!"

Mike nodded. As Colin's team took the field for the final inning, Mike jumped up, pumped his fist, and yelled, "Go, Cooperstown!"

"They're going to do it!" Mike said. "I can just feel it!"

Cooperstown's Logan Fogg was on the mound for the sixth inning. He was lights out. Nobody could stop him! He struck out the first Chula Vista player on three pitches. He got the second Chula Vista player to ground out to third.

As Fogg stood on the mound facing the third Chula Vista hitter, the Cooperstown fans in the stands went wild, clapping and yelling. Mike and Kate jumped and joined in.

"Go, Cooperstown!" Mike called.

"You got him, Fogg!" Kate screamed.

Logan Fogg threw a fastball.

The Chula Vista batter swung.

TWAP!

The ball sailed high into the air. The Chula Vista batter scrambled for first. The ball sailed over the shortstop's head. The Cooperstown fans instantly grew quiet. It was as if everyone in Lamade Stadium was holding their breath.

The Chula Vista batter ran for second. The ball flew into the outfield. The centerfielder ran back toward the outfield wall. The Chula Vista runner tagged second base. The ball started to drop. The runner headed for third.

PLOP!

The ball fell into the centerfielder's glove! It was an out! The inning was over!

Cooperstown had won the game!

Mike, Kate, and all the Cooperstown fans burst into cheers and yells.

"They did it!" Mike said.

"Talk about Big Daddy Hacks!" Kate said. "That was a great game!"

Out on the field, Coach Caleb was mobbed by his team. They bounced up and down and patted his head. Coach Caleb motioned to the dugout. A moment later, Zach ran out onto the field. The players surrounded him and cheered just as the TV cameras arrived. They circled around the Cooperstown team as the players hoisted Zach on their shoulders and cheered, "Hip, hip, hooray!" The cameras took close-ups of Zach and the rest of the team.

The celebration continued for some time. But eventually the umpires shooed Cooperstown from the field. The players grabbed their equipment and headed for the exit.

Kate and Mike had been watching it all from their seats. "Come on," Kate said. "Let's go meet up with the team!"

She and Mike raced through Lamade Stadium and out into the bright sunshine. They waited near the gate to the field as Cooperstown exited. Mike and Kate gave high fives as one player after another went by. "Good game!" they called out.

Mike and Kate cheered loudly as Colin passed by. He stopped for a moment in front of them and took off his baseball cap. "You know," he said, "being at the Little League World Series isn't about winning. I'm really happy just to be playing here. But I have to say, winning does feel pretty good!"

"Woo-hoo!" Mike yelled. He gave Colin a fist bump, then Colin ran to catch up with his teammates.

Mike and Kate were just about to leave when they spotted Zach at the end of the line.

"Hey!" Zach said. "Hang on!" He jogged over to them. "I wanted to thank you," he said. "The last few hours have been amazing. You helped me realize that the best legacy I can leave is to help others. Thank you!"

Mike and Kate looked at each other and smiled.

"You're welcome," Kate said. "Now you're talking like a *real* hero!"

Dugout Notes

☆ The World Series Kids ☆

A league for kids. Little League Baseball and Softball is run by Little League International. They're based in South Williamsport, Pennsylvania, near where the organization was founded. Millions of boys and girls play Little League Baseball and Softball each year around the world.

A big little series. The Little League Baseball World Series is played each August in South Williamsport. Local baseball leagues pick their best players for an all-star team. The best team in each state goes to a regional tournament, made up of multiple states. There are eight regions in the United States and eight international ones. The winners in each region head to the Little League World Series. Starting from the local playoffs, more than 16,000 baseball games are played over 45 days to determine the best team in the world!

A founder. Carl Stotz was the founder of Little League. In 1938, while playing with his nephews, he had the idea for a baseball league designed for kids. That summer, he organized local boys and tried out different equipment and field designs. It was Stotz who came up with the sixty-foot distance between bases. The first Little League game was played on June 6, 1939. The first three teams were Lycoming Dairy, Lundy Lumber, and Jumbo Pretzel!

World Series stadiums. The Little League Baseball World Series games are played at Lamade or Volunteer Stadiums in South Williamsport. Lamade Stadium and the outfield berm can hold up to 40,000 fans. That's as many as some major-league stadiums! The second stadium at the Little League Baseball World Series complex is Volunteer Stadium. It can hold 5,000 fans.

We're on TV! The Little League Baseball World Series has been nationally televised since 1963. More recently, the eight regional tournaments have been covered, too.

Everyone can play. Little League has a division for players with physical or intellectual challenges. Each year, the Challenger Division has an exhibition game at Volunteer Stadium during the Little League Baseball World Series.

Colorful pins. Pin collecting and trading is a big activity for the players and fans at the Little League Baseball World Series. The first official pin was issued in 1983. Both players and fans collect and trade pins. There are official Little League pins, but businesses, teams, and even individuals can create and trade their own pins. Some fans have thousands of pins!

Girls making the play. Unfortunately, girls were banned from Little League and the Little League Baseball World Series until 1974. Now girls can play in both! In 2014, Mo'ne Davis became the first girl to pitch a winning game and to pitch a shutout in the Little League Baseball World Series. It was such an accomplishment that she was the first Little League Baseball player to be featured on the cover of *Sports Illustrated* magazine.

A ticket to the majors. Some Little League Baseball World Series players have made it to the major leagues, including Gary Sheffield and Cody Bellinger. So far, only three major-league players (Ed

Vosberg, Jason Varitek, and Michael Conforto) have played in the Little League Baseball World Series final, the College World Series final, and the Major League Baseball World Series.

Real international champions. The first team from another country to win the Little League Baseball World Series was a team from Monterrey, Mexico, in 1957. The team worked incredibly hard and made sacrifices to travel to the World Series. Nobody expected them to win, but they beat the United States team from

La Mesa, California. Their pitcher, Angel Macias, threw a perfect game (that means he pitched the whole game and didn't allow any player to reach first base)! Hundreds of thousands of fans cheered for them when the team returned to Mexico.

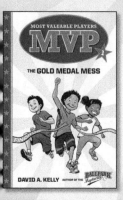
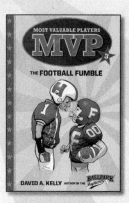

New friends. New adventures.
Find a new series . . . just for you!

ISADORA MOON

For ballerina and fairy and vampire lovers

COMMANDER IN CHEESE

For adventurers

JULIAN'S WORLD
THE STORIES JULIAN TELLS

For storytellers

PUPPY PIRATES

For dog lovers

PuRRmaids

For mermaid and cat lovers

BALLPARK Mysteries

For sports fans

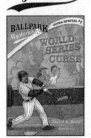

RHCB **RHCBooks.com**